THERE WAS AN OLD LADY WHO SWALLOWED A FROG!

by Lucille Colandro
Illustrated by Jared Lee

Cartwheel Books

an imprint of Scholastic Inc.

For Rita, who loves to garden and all our future blossoms—
Annabelle, Hattie, Karzi, Kaitlyn, Roberta, and Violet.
Love, L.C.

To Jenny Berberich
—J.L.

ISBN 978-0-545-83213-7

12 11 10 9 8 7 6 5 4 3 2 1   15 16 17 18 19 20/0

Printed in the U.S.A.   40
This edition first printing, January 2015

There was an old lady who swallowed a frog.
I don't know why she swallowed the frog.
She was in a fog.

There was an old lady who swallowed some dirt.
It didn't hurt to swallow that dirt.

She swallowed the dirt to hide the frog.
I don't know why she swallowed the frog.
She was in a fog.

There was an old lady who swallowed some seeds.
At high speeds, she swallowed the seeds.

She swallowed the seeds to fill in the dirt.
She swallowed the dirt to hide the frog.

I don't know why she swallowed the frog.
She was in a fog.

There was an old lady who swallowed the rain.

What did she gain by swallowing the rain?

She swallowed the rain to water the seeds.
She swallowed the seeds to fill in the dirt.
She swallowed the dirt to hide the frog.

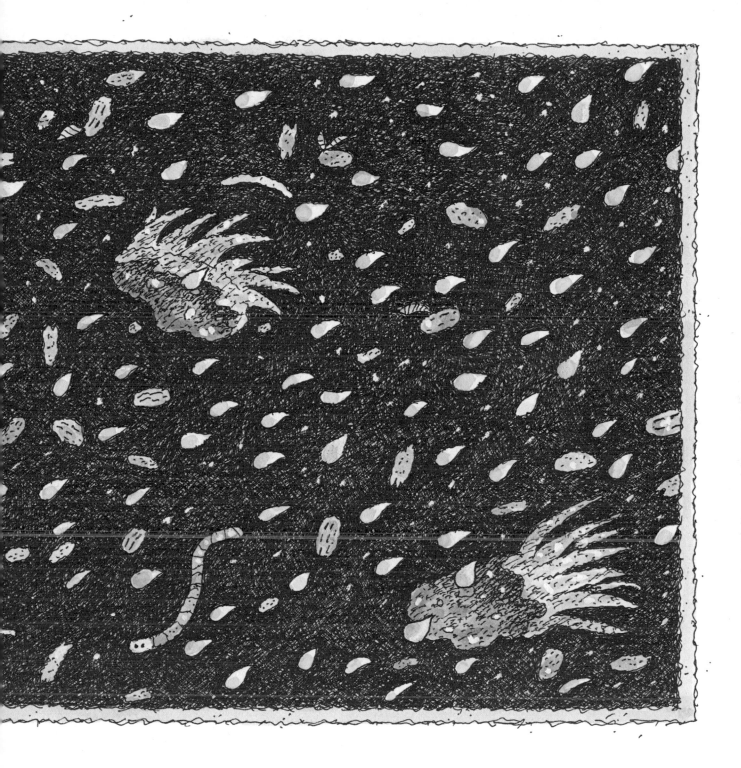

I don't know why she swallowed the frog.
She was in a fog.

There was an old lady who swallowed the sunlight.

It was so fun, right? To swallow the sunlight.

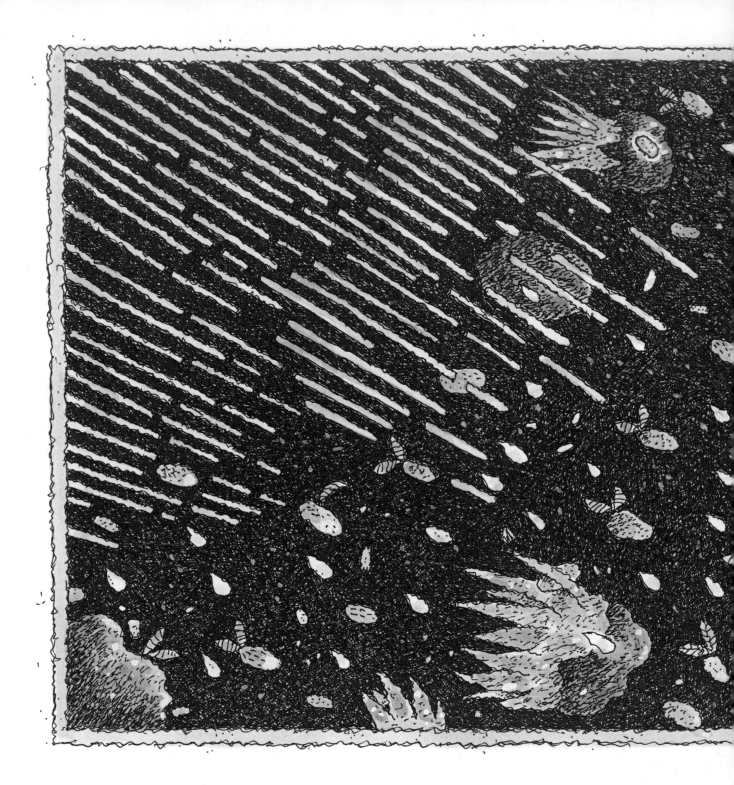

She swallowed the sunlight to dry up the rain.
She swallowed the rain to water the seeds.
She swallowed the seeds to fill in the dirt.

She swallowed the dirt to hide the frog.
I don't know why she swallowed the frog.
She was in a fog.

There was an old lady who swallowed some gloves.
Oh, how she loves to swallow her gloves.

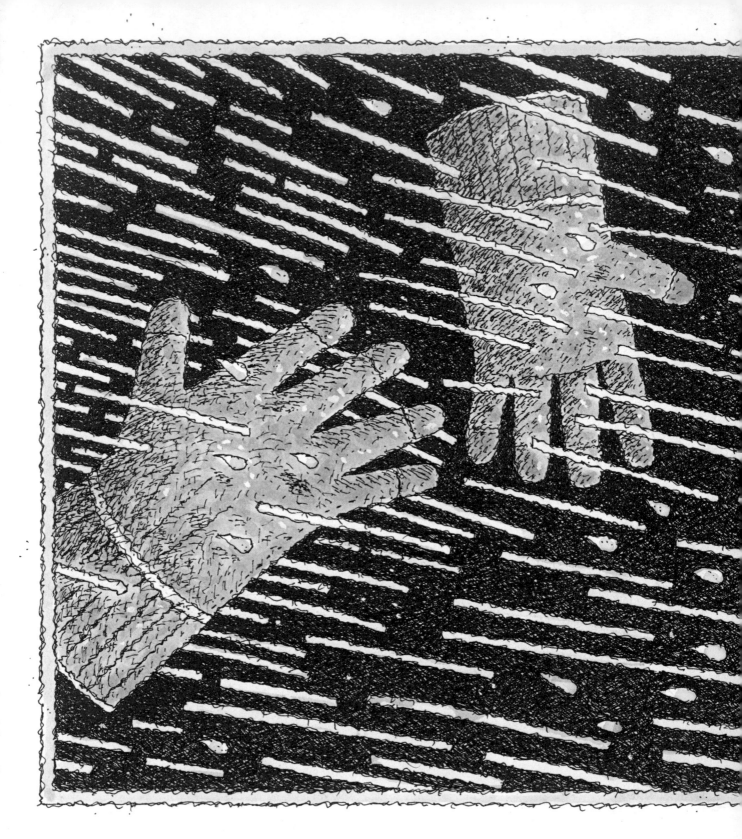

She swallowed the gloves to hold the sunlight.

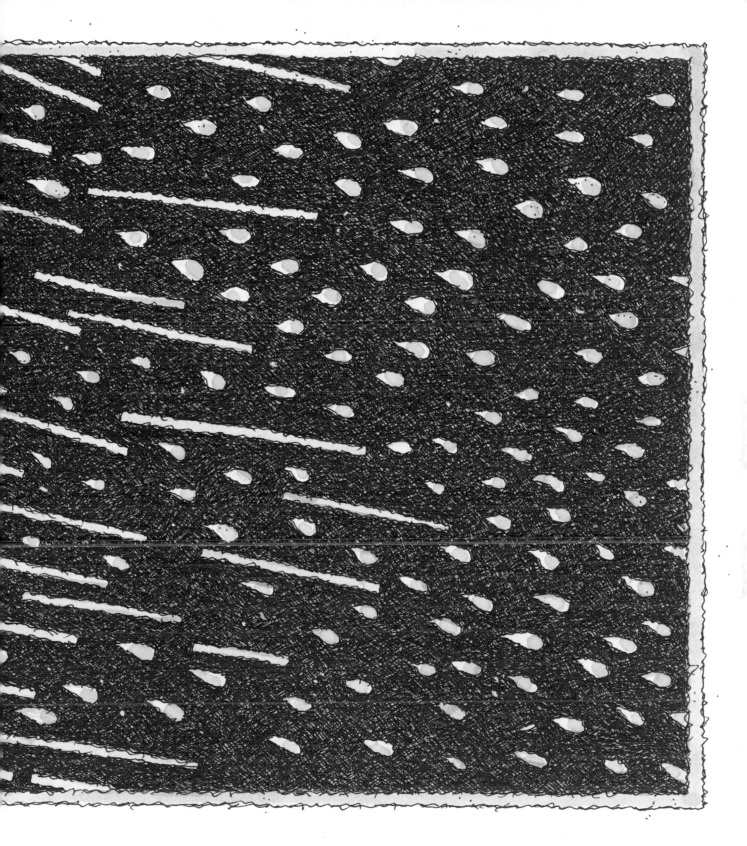

She swallowed the sunlight to dry up the rain.

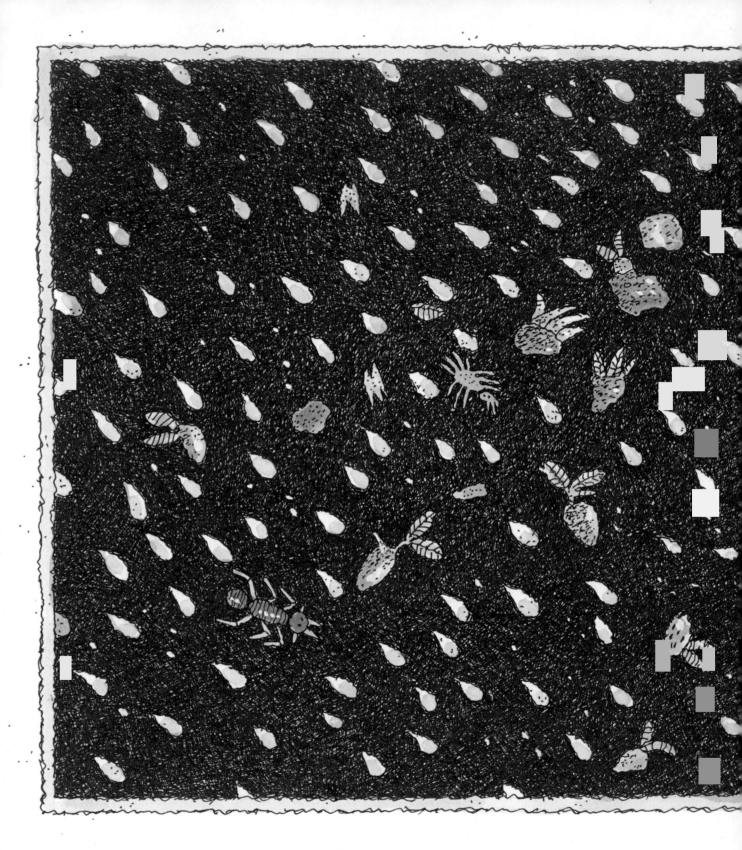

She swallowed the rain to water the seeds.

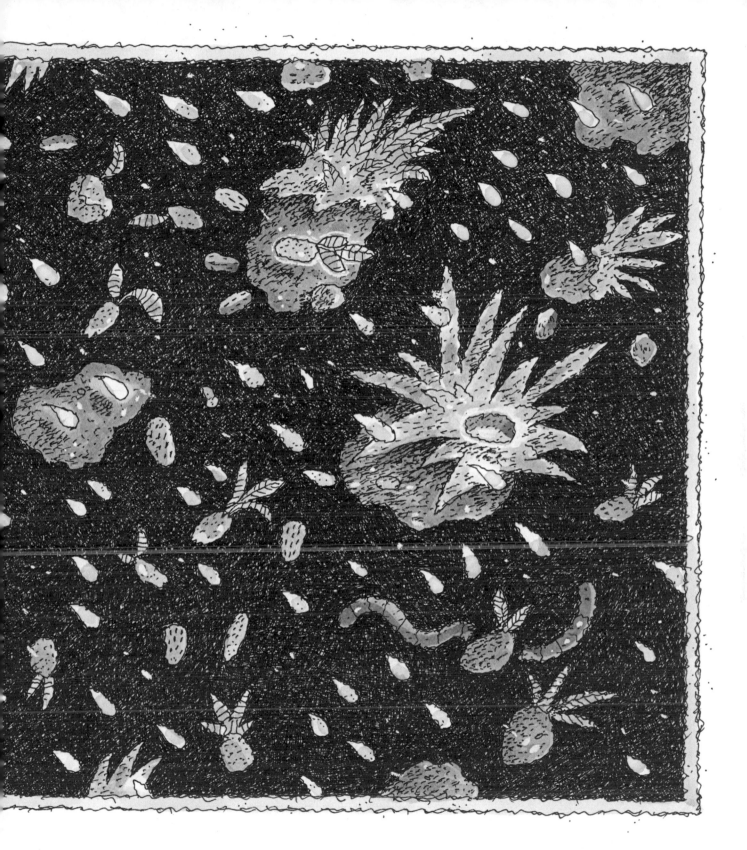

She swallowed the seeds to fill in the dirt.

She swallowed the dirt to hide the frog.

I don't know why she swallowed the frog.
She was in a fog.

There was an old lady who swallowed a rake.

It was a mistake to swallow that rake!

So the old lady said, "Excuse me! I beg your pardon . . ."

... and out spilled a colorful garden!

Happy spring!